LOVE IN OTHER REALMS

poetry & prose
MELISSA M. COMBS

"Beareth all things, believeth all things,
hopeth all things, endureth all things."

- 1 Corinthians 13:7

LOVE ☆

IN OTHER REALMS

If we are to live life in harmony with the universe,
we must all possess the powerful faith in what
the ancients used to call "fatum,"
what we currently refer to as destiny."

— Jeremy Piven, *Serendipity*

Dedicated to **you**, the reader.

I hope that you get a chance to feel it all — l o v e and all
of it's many seasons. The way that it first feels to levitate just
inches off of the ground. To float and then to soar.
But also what it feels like to crash, if only just once
in your lifetime. To find it in you to create some kind of art
or poetry as deep as your scars and as free flowing as
the blood from the wounds that they once were.
To witness, for the first time in your life,
the beautiful, awe-inspiring strength that has and always
will exist within you,
as you are scattered ashes, reforming in infinite wind.
And when the darkest night of your soul arrives,
I pray that you find what you have always sought after —
l o v e , the truth, and the light.

With all of my love,
Melissa.

Love

ALONE

IS

PROOF

THAT

THERE

ARE

OTHER

REALMS.

there was this to ponder,
he was either the *l o v e* of my life—
the one whom i had roamed
all of heaven and earth
in search of,
or a muse, sent by the angels,
to catapult me out of my
former destruction.

but either way i saw it,
it was ultimately him that saved me.

and for that,
what other choice did i have
but to *l o v e* him?

if when it's over
they are still the lyrics to your favorite songs
and they are in every detail of your dreams,
both in waking and in sleep,
then what you had with them was *real.*

and just remember,
nothing real in this life ever dies,
it only changes form.

from the moment
you took hold of my hand
i sensed the beginning
of a lifelong journey —
mysteries begging to
be solved,
hidden truths waiting
to be unveiled,
and an ancient world
dying to be understood.

you were then and you are now
more than mere human to me.
you are proof of the purest immortality;
l o v e here and *now*
and *l o v e* in all lifetimes to come.

only god could have
planned something
so brilliant…
me meeting you.
you —
the only soul capable
of waking
me from an eternity
of sleep.

truthfully,
the more time that i spend
in this tainted and fallen
world,
the more i understand
that a *l o v e* like yours and
mine is meant for something
larger than ourselves.

how fickle, to *l o v e* ,
only for the romance,
when everything that could comes of this;
of us, is powerful enough to
reshape our very world.

you are my 'after',
the pivotal shift in my life;
the moment where *everything* changed.

i just need to know
 that you and i
exist outside of our bodies—

that i could
 close my eyes
    and
 meet you
        anytime
            and *anywhere.*

need i ever question
whether or not there
is a god above,
or whether or not
is a waste of one's soul
to have hope,
i shall simply close my eyes
and remember the way that the sky
once cracked open—
the universe revealing itself
and all of it's glory to you and i…
if only for a brief moment in time.

i have this notion that
together we would radiate
a *l o v e* so powerful that it
would shock the world's system—
burning so brightly
within one another's arms
that even the night's sky
would mistake us as his stars.

when i am in alignment with you,
  somehow i am connected to all that surrounds me.

and they tell me that you and i
will always find one another
in our future lifetimes to come.
but i don't want you
only in future lifetimes to come.
i want you *now* and i want you
for all of *eternity*.

all of you, intertwined
with all of me, until we merge as one,
forevermore;
until neither life nor death
can do us part.

LOVING HIM IS KNOWING THAT I

WOULD BUY A ONE WAY TICKET

TO HELL IF IT MEANT BEING

WITH HIM, BUT KNOWING

WITH ALL OF MY HEART

THAT OUR LOVE IS OF

HEAVEN AND GUIDED

INFINITELY BY

THE HANDS

OF OUR

FATHER.

i can't be one of them,
the all is doomed, all is lost,
faithless ones.

not having met him.
not having seen the world behind
the veil of what the eyes can see.
and especially not having felt what
i have felt, both in his arms and
far from reach.

and still the final picture remains
a blur; the story of us; my life; him…

all i know is that i just i can't—
i *can't* be one of them.

i'm not in search of much...

only another whom my soul
is entirely *free* to escape my body
in front of.

separation does one of two things —
it either allows you the time to move forward,
or it reveals to you the ever present tug and
longing of your heart,
for what *was*, what still *is*,
and what will *always* be.

still i crave you in unnatural ways,
as if i am the waves wishing to abandon
the shore to marry the sky.

how it is that our souls find
another in which they are
magnetized to above 7.8 billion
other souls still remains the greatest
mystery to me.

it's like no matter how many
others cross our paths along the way,
none have the power to break
the pulling energy of the one to
whom our souls belong.

they tell me to bury the story
of you and i,
as if we are some sort of body
that can easily be killed and
disposed of;
as if we are an entity of only
frail and human mortality…

as if we are not one in spirit,
and as if *love* could ever die.

" *l o v e* you always,"
he said.

only a few short words.
it wasn't like it was
poetry or anything.

but see, that's the thing…
with him,
it never had to be.
with him, all things,
even what some would consider
trivial,
they were monumental
to me.

the purest *l o v e* is like a glacier of ice
when put through fire.
it may melt and it may in fact change form,
but never is it separated
and *never* is it lost.

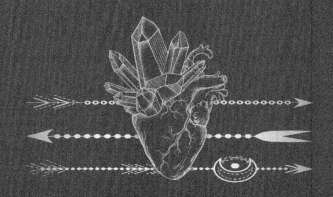

and now i know
that to walk away
from our
connection
would be to
sever my
own soul;

to free me
of the burden
of this heavy
pain,
but also
to rob me
of one of the deepest
l o v e s , that i,
in this lifetime,
have
ever known.

it's sad
but beautiful
really…
the woman who
walks alone
after her heartbreak.

sad, because there
is no one nor thing
powerful enough
to distract
her from her pain.

beautiful,
because her
grief is heavy
and her *love*
proven pure.

an open letter to the unknown:

guide me through your throat's tunnel
and if needed swallow me whole…

so long as in the darkness of your belly
i return to my beloved in both the *flesh*
and in the *soul*.

without searching,
i find you.
without reaching,
i feel you.
without asking,
i know you.

we have always been
one, split into two,
destined to find our way
back to one another,
in this walk of life
and in all walks to come.

the truth is,
we wouldn't fear living a life lost
had we another hand to hold —
one that we could count on to
never let ours go.

in my world,
the ninety nine
would leave when
i asked them to.
they would see the
walls as wounds
and they would run so far
that the soles of
their shoes burn out.

in my world,
only *the one* would stay.

let us not forget the waves
as they reach for the heavens,
that it is only natural of them...

and that so too is my reach for you.

darling,
be the waves
if you must.
pull away in pain
and then come
violently
crashing down.

be unsure.
get angry.
transform into
a tsunami.

i will remain the shore —
still; every grain of sand
longing for your embrace.

to *l o v e* unrequited
is far from weakness.

despite the foolish
whispers of the world,
you are one of the strongest
creations known to
existence;
the force that
keeps our very world
spinning.

and if at the end of it all i am left only with one belief—
the belief that fate is in favor of us...
then i am left with all that i will ever need.

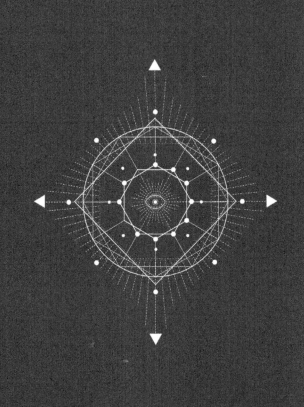

i trust in the alchemy of heaven,
that if you are in fact meant for me
as the signs have so persistently claimed,
then you will, in divine timing,
find your way back to me.

and there is nothing in this world
that i could ever do
to hinder this,
to speed this up,
to manipulate this,
or to lose this.

and now when i hear someone say
"i feel lost without them…"
i get it.
i whole heartedly get it.
because the worst kind of lost
that one can be
is not in the physical but in the spiritual.

and when our other halves go missing,
we venture off, relentlessly in search.
often times without a compass,
a map,
or even so much as a light.

and to wilderness,
we roam.

and *we roam.*
and *we roam.*
and *we roam.*

"nothing worth anything
ever comes easy in this life,"
they say.

but *you* —
you came easy.
and you are worth *everything* to me.

my tears
were encrypted
messages to his
higher self.
i wasn't just crying
to heal,
i was crying to
communicate
to the heavens
and to him —

return
to
me.

believing in what
we cannot see —
some call it foolish.

those of us paying attention…
we call it *faith*.

something about this deja vu
tells me that i have lived this life before;
that i will *always* find my way
back to you.

when i close my eyes
i can *feel* you,
more than the sheets that i lie
beneath
and even more than this air
that i breathe.

climbing
out of my body to meet
you becomes easier
the more time passes
and the more distance
grows between.

(the classic tale of
l o v e refusing the command
of the physical.)

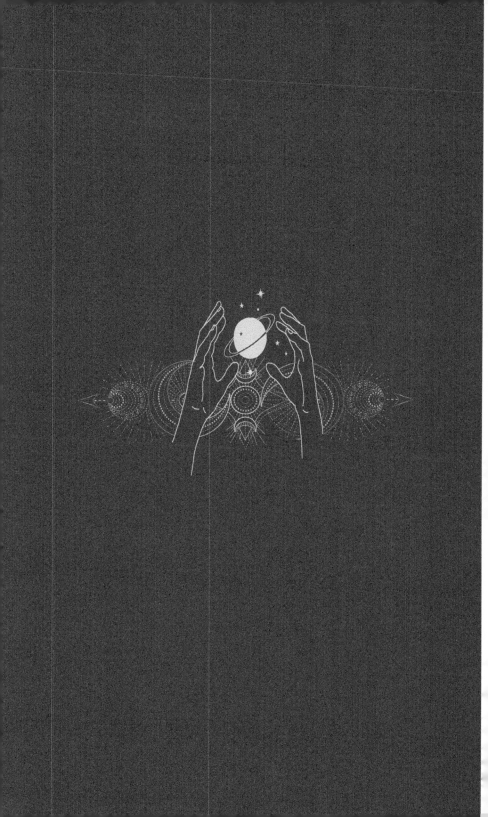

after all of
this time
the tears still
show up now and again
to remind me that what
i had for you was real.

and i'm learning to
welcome them;
reminding myself
that it is okay to *feel.*

we could run off
to somewhere
far away from here;
travel highways
without speed limits;
levitate off of the ground,
just high enough to escape
all of their rules.

anywhere but here,
so long as i am *with you.*

and just like that
time stood still
and it was you and
i together
in all of the ways that
i had ever previously dreamt.

and i knew then,
in that moment,
that manifestation
was more than fairytale,
but law.
and that you and i were more
than a meaningless chance,
but a sacred and holy destiny.

if your capacity
to love has yet to
grow,

then i wish our story to
be
as flesh
stabbed by thorns;
to endure the pain
as i *l o v e* you for
all that you are.

LOVE IN OTHER REALMS
75

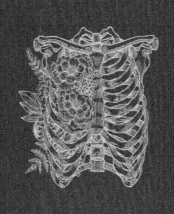

for lifetimes i have been
stripped bare;
my rib cage robbed of it's support;
merciless rejection on a mission to destroy me.

be the one to gently repaint my walls;
carve the language of *l o v e* into the depths
of my soul and build me
once and for all into a home.

if i did in fact
manifest you
into existence,
then in essence,
i am your creator.

therefore, let me *l o v e*
you as my creation,
holding you close inside
of arms that long
to never let you go.

a *l o v e* like yours and mine
is no freak accident.

we are a messy, yet beautiful,
pre-destined collision.

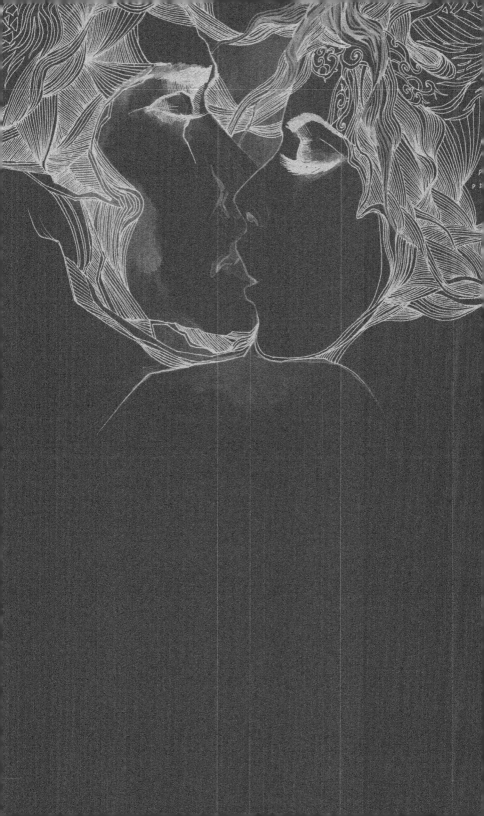

once you have learned
that *l o v e*
is metaphysical above
all else,
not even the most
convincing
seperation
nor the most intimidating
distance can keep the two
of you apart.

it was you.

all along, it was you that i was writing for.

before my eyes had ever set sight on you,
every cell making up the composition
of my body,
they knew you.

i had to say no

to so many things

in order to find you.

while drowning in our memories
i have learned that viewing the rays
of the sun from beneath the waves
is a lot like looking into a kaleidoscope —

it's a breathtakingly beautiful distortion.

and for that,
i will *always* choose to stay.

the longer i live this
life without you,
the heavier the burden
grows.

but maybe that is why god
allows you to travel into
my dreams these days…
so that sleep may be the
necessary rest not only for
my body,
but for my aching heart
and soul.

i'm not asking for much…
only that when you leave
you might let me hold
you from afar.

there are many things
that i am willing to let go of in
this lifetime.

but you and what we have
will never be one of them.

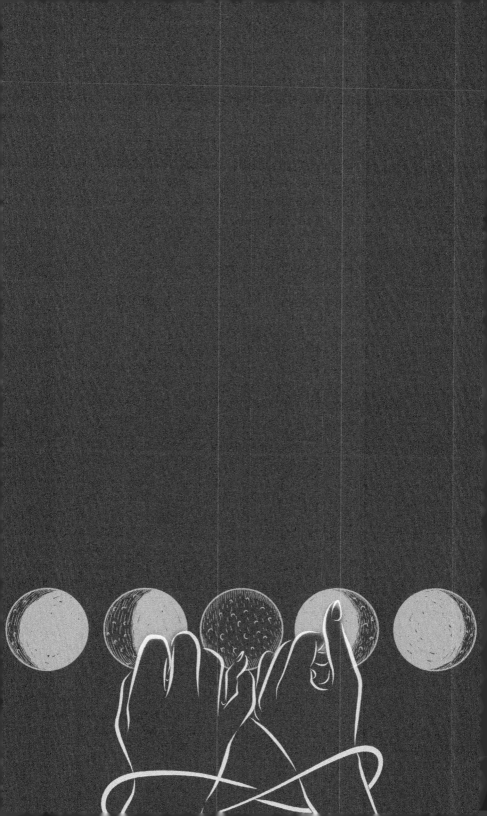

falling in *l o v e* with an angel
is easy;
effortless,
even.

but a fallen angel?
without mercy, the experience
will wind you tightly within
it's grip,
commanding you to shatter
until you are but micro shards
upon the cold and unforgiving
grounds of hell.

it is pain like no other…
and it is sacrifice like no other.

but ultimately…
it is *l o v e* like no other.

for it asks of you these two questions:
"can you *l o v e* ,
without condition?"
and "do you stand strong in
your faith of restoration?"

and if you can in fact answer yes
to the two, then the keys to the kingdom
will soon be handed to you.

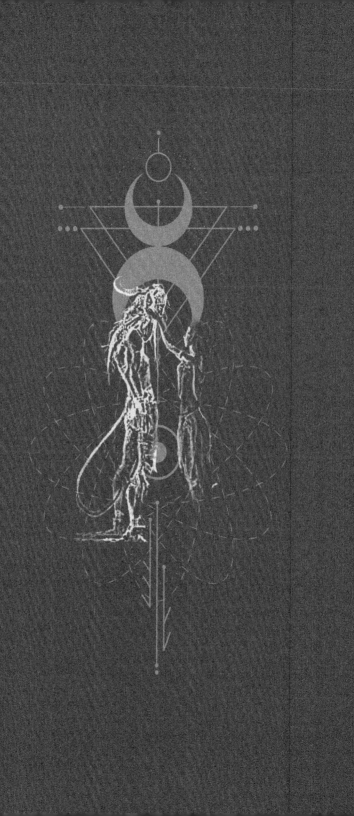

god knows that i could hate
you right now…
for having me fall like never before;
for making me desire you the way
that i desire my very next breath…
and worse,
for leaving me
to find my own way out of this
purgatory hell, otherwise known as
life without you.

and yet still
with all of the pain that has taken
residence inside of me,
there is always room left for these
three worlds , 'i *l o v e* you.'

they would have been
enough for me…
before knowing you;
before learning
that there is more
substance to be
found in *l o v e*.

and now, in knowing this,
i would spend ninety
years alone
if it meant spending
my very last with you.

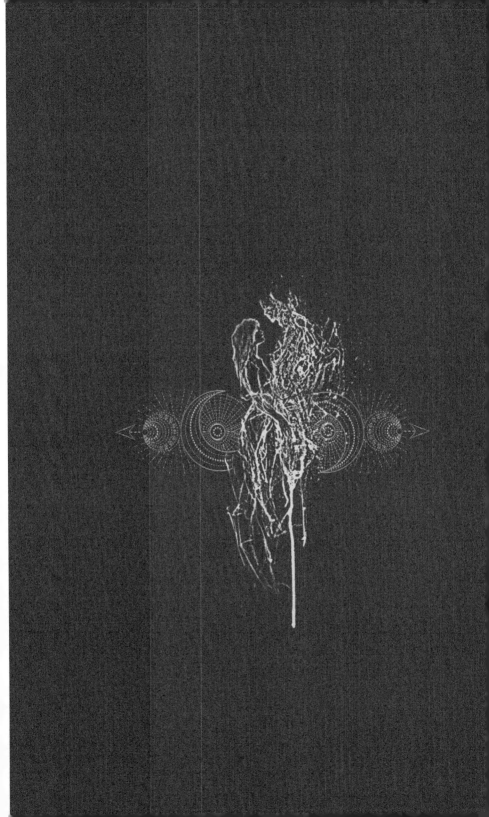

this is how i hold onto you—
as if i have fallen ship,
water -2.2 degrees celsius
and you are the one
and only piece of ice
left to hold onto;
the only possibility of
preservation until dry land.

who were the parts of me
that you set out to disintegrate?
who is she
that lies as ashes at your feet?
from where was she born
and to where does she descend?
may i care no more.

who am i,
i ask...
the one awakening, and to where
will i ascend?

on which planet shall i meet you?
to where will we travel and to whom
the glory do we owe?
may this be all i ever care to know.

from the moment that you and i
were born onto this earth,
our contracts were created,
stating "destined to meet;
by law, to *l o v e*."

signed, god.

so it turns out
that the tale of true *l o v e s* first
kiss is far from myth.

for you*r l o v e* awakened
me
to all that was dead
inside of me.

am i thankful for the gift
of second sight?
of course.

but there are just
some things that this
telepathy cannot replace...
like the way you
would transfer your thoughts
from your finger tips
unto my thighs.
or what about the mornings
that i would
awaken to your lips
lightly pressed in
between the blades
of my shoulders?

this *l o v e* is greater than i
have ever known—
to *l o v e* one another from within.

but some nights, i simply miss
the magic of your touch
and the beauty, that is your skin.

how do you know if you've found the one?

believe me when i tell you this.
when you have found the one…
questions like these need not to be asked.

and now i am most
certain that a forever
without you
is the 'eternity in hell'
that the scriptures have
spoken of.

forgive me.

there is no *l o v e* to be found
in the wading of shallow waters,
this i have learned.

it is stepping out unto troubled waters,
risking the fall into complete and total
submersion...

only to learn that
now
you can walk on water.

they say that as an empath
i have a hard time seeing the
bad in people
because i am too busy
giving credit to all of their good;
that by now
i should have seen you for
who you truly are;
that i should have left.

but of them,
i ask,
is empathy not greater
than apathy;
and *l o v e* not stronger than hate?

you'll meet that one person
in life and suddenly it will become
unfair to every other person
from there on out...
because in between the smiles
and all of the laughter held
with someone new,
the ghost of that one person
will always be there,
wining and dining,
making *l o v e* to,
and tempting your every thought.

l o v e s magnetic pull is as pure as it is
supernatural —
calling us to put our hearts on the line;
begging us to dive the depths.

and ultimately, to be rewarded.

some enter your life as a spark,
others, a flame.

but there is only one
that will act as your baptism
by fire,
transforming you from the inside out,
for all of time.

i don't mind you setting fire
to my soul
so long as you will be there
as the sculptor
when i am the ashes
in need of sculpting.

just for tonight
the thought of falling asleep
underneath the same stars is
enough for me.

but i know and god knows
and all of the angels,
they know too...
that as i awaken tomorrow
morning, i am right back
to my longing and searching
for you.

losing you taught me
the construct of time
and even the holiness
of a moment,
whether it be
at the time
perceived as 'good'
or as 'bad'.

because when you
l o v e someone...
when you *truly l o v e*
someone
and they are no
longer around...
any memory becomes
treasure
in the treasure box
that we call the mind.

from where i am standing,
your body's frame
is but a spec;
blurry to the point of
an eye strain;
distorted severely,
as to pose the thought,
'is it really even you?';
and a blanket of fog
covering you, from
head to toe.

my eyes catch the glimpse
needed, just barely.

and it is always that 'just barely'
that keeps my focus on you.

she said, "i'm not coming back down to earth
until i manifest all of what belongs to me,
starting with *h i m*
and ending with all of *e t e r n i t y* ."

if there are forces keeping you from me,
tell them that the battle may be their's…

but the war is *mine*.

the *l o v e* that i have for you is so
overwhelming
that even my words fail at accurately
conveying it.

and yet everyday, still i try.
pages as a wishing well for my tears to fall;
blood as my ink;
hours and hours, days, weeks, months,
and years...

all in the hopes that you may
one day inquire of and requite
my *l o v e* for you.

you are like the molecules of air
in so many ways —
invisible, yet in constant
effect to the world around me.

and no matter how many times
i breathe you out,
inevitably, i must breathe you
back in.

i stopped fully living in
this world
the day that i learned of
you and of *us*
and of the inner realm
that we now share.

my eyes have seen far too much
for me to entertain the idea that life is
just a random series of
meaningless events.

and by my eyes seeing
far too much,
i mean that my eyes saw *him*.

it's hard enough to give up on love, as is.

for those of us witness to the magic of a miracle...
it is nearly impossible.

it's crazy the way that one source
can have you both as a feather floating
weightlessly in the wind

and as a rock so heavily weighed down
in the river
that even the current refuses to take
you with it.

(me with you vs. me without you.)

in slow motion
and yet seemingly all at once,
he had become my favorite escape
from the darkness that this world
had lain.

all i had to do was close my eyes,
and every time it was *him and i* —

no violence.
no death.
no injustice,
nor evil reign.

just *him and i*,
and only this to remain.

of all the paths
that this life has to offer,
i pray your roads traveled
always lead you back to me.

l o v e them through
all of their madness
and all of their darkness.

why?

because *l o v e* was never
promised to be easy.

as god's
daughter, it
is only
natural that
i too
love you at
your *darkest*.

to be loved
i believe
is to be embraced,
to be reassured,
and to be pursued,
while simultaneously
being allowed to roam
free.

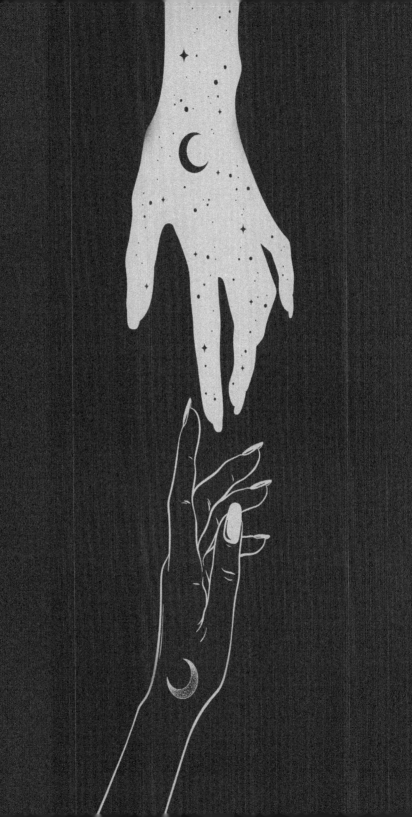

even in the midst of space
my arms stretch out for you;
my heart *yearns* for you.

when i told you that i loved you,
i spoke that into existence for all
of eternity.
and when i told you that i would
never let you go,
what that meant is that i am
fighting all of hell just to bring
you home.

since the beginning of time
there has been a question that
people have died to learn the
answer to —
a question far more fascinating
than all of the rest.

that question is...
"what is *l o v e ?*"

and while there is only
one answer to this question,
there are many ways
that it can be described.

for me,
l o v e is someone who forces
you to get uncomfortable;
someone who forces you to
let go of your yesterdays to
pursue your tomorrows,
without limitation.

l o v e isn't always a calm breeze
that awaits you in the morning,
comforting you at the start of your
every day.

sometimes *l o v e* is a scorching
flame that sets your soul on fire.
and yes,
when it burns,
it is undoubtedly uncomfortable.

but you know what else *l o v e* is?
l o v e is the grace hiding behind
that very flame.
l o v e is the force that encourages
you to grow,
rather than to remain the same.

and it is not that *love* does not
appreciate you for who you are.
only the contrary.
it *loves* you so much that it
recognizes that you were
destined to become more.

love comforts you,
while simultaneously pushing you.
love finds you face down in the dirt
and before you know it,
you have taken flight and you are
soaring past the older and weaker
version of you.

you see,
love knows when to hold your hand
but also when to let go to watch you
conquer things on your own.

love knows how to give you space,
while seeing to it that you never feel alone.

love —
it is the force that carries you
through
the darkness, all the while,
making you feel at home.

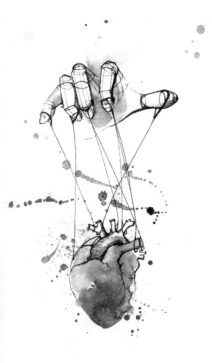

i'm tired of going where i am
told to go and being with who
i am told to be with. i want to go
where it feels *right*
and i want to be
with whom my
soul tells me to be with.

"would it really kill you if we kissed?"
he asked.

to his response:
"if there is anything in this world
worth dying for,
it is this, a perfect *l o v e* ."

i had felt butterflies many of times
and i had grown quite familiar with
the law of excitement and unfamiliarity;
the anticipation of merging with another.
i had felt everything under the sun,
i had believed...

until i laid my eyes on him.
until i was held within his arms.

suddenly,
i had learned that there were more
than butterflies in this great big world.
there were these majestic birds,
composed entirely of fire.

and that day
i learned that while butterflies make a
home inside of your heart,
birds of fire make a home of
your entire soul.

he asked,
"if i had told you from the beginning
that i was fire… would you have still loved me?"

when your *l o v e* for them
surpasses human reasoning…
i hope you finally believe in
life after death
and in the kingdom to come.

because that is,
in fact,
where your new understanding
has come from.

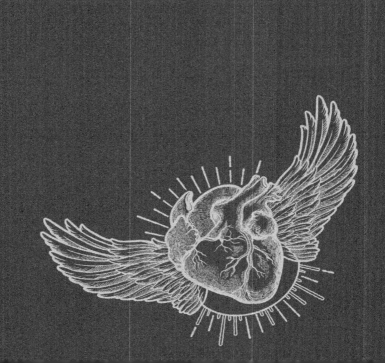

i could never care what
others think of my *l o v e* for you,
for it was faith that first led me
into your arms;
it was stepping into the unknown
so that i could receive this —
a *l o v e* far greater than what
the eyes can see;
a *l o v e* that required sacrifice
and selflessness.

and for the first time in my life,
a *l o v e* that demanded my guard
to be let down.

if it is hell that i must fight
to keep you here,
then tell the demons to
armor up.

because as far as i am
concerned,
it would take far less
energy to fight for you,
than it would to let you go.

how about this…
i give, give, give,
and you
take, take, take,
until all of my *l o v e*
fills up your holes
and you have some in
turn that you may finally
give away.

and then you will bury
your head into my shoulder
once more
and whisper,
"i will no longer allow you
to go on living this way."

then you and i,
we'll own the night
and all of the stars,
the sunshine and all
of the rain.
hearts set free at last…
and no longer
will we owe our debts
to the bondage of pain.

and so *this isn't goodbye.*
this is the realization that
our souls have been eternally
tied;
the moment in time where
i vow to always pray for you,
to wish you the best,
and to *l o v e* you in all of the
ways refused by the rest.

you are the one that i am in training for...

the soul that i would die to set *free*.

it's one thing to miss
someone on the hard days.
it's an entirely different
thing to miss them
when all is going
well.

because, it is in those moments
you realize that you miss them
out of *l o v e* ,
not out of desperation.

they could hang the moon for me…
but they'll never be *you*.

it's the way that i feel you without
seeing you,
and the way that i hear you,
without you so much as
murmuring a word.
gets me every time.

as a young girl
i remember watching
a scene in a movie where jesus bled from a cross
for the very ones who nailed him to it.
and i might not have understood at the
time why...
but i at least learned in that moment never to
assume that *l o v e* would be easy...
only that sacrifice
was beautiful, and that *l o v e* , in the end,
is always worth it.

as we were not of this world,
nor was our *l o v e* for one another.

to an outsider,
l o v e can make
someone appear
to have gone crazy.

but to the one
experiencing
l o v e,
it is the only time that
they have ever truly
felt sane.

here's the thing,
i could learn that you never
even loved me the way that you
claimed to…

but it wouldn't prevent me from
loving you.
because it was never about your *l o v e*
for me,
but mine for you.

l o v e is without condition
or none at all.
thats it.

no "but—"
no "what if—?"
no nothing.

without condition,
or
none
at
all.

LOVE IN OTHER REALMS
171

i prayed, "give me something worth writing
about and even more than that,
something worth living for."

...*and there you were.*

i've watched seconds develop
into minutes and minutes into hours,
and just as easily, days into years...
yet still in the midst of time escaping me,
your memory lingers
with supernatural vibrancy.

and now i know that 'falling in *l o v e* '
is more than mere figure of speech.

walked in tall and proud
and came vulnerably
crashing to my knees.

i wonder
if in my realm sleep
i toss and turn just right,
could i possibly bring you
back into the natural
world with me?

please?

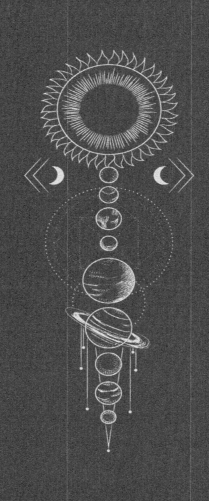

when it comes to *l o v e* ,
the hands of time mean absolutely nothing.
you proved that to me.

some souls, we meet, and that very
first touch is the hole that we fall
head over heels into.

i can't tell if the
highways are even
highways anymore.
they feel more
like teleports
into endless thoughts
of you.

i don't find it to be fair,
hearing them say that
in letting you go
i will set myself free.

what part, i wonder,
do they not
understand, when i say
that with you was the
only time in my life
that i ever did feel free.

when i listen to the stories
of others
and the peaceful promises
of letting go…
for a moment, it tempts me
as the easier route.

but then i remember
the wisdom of the ancient
texts… that often times
the hardest paths are the
most fulfilling.

and once more, i stay.
i will *always* choose to stay.

you make it clear to me
that *l o v e* is the greatest risk that we will ever take,

but that in not taking it
we risk even more.

an angel asked of me,
"do you believe that the signs
were always pointing to him?"

i said,
"from the moment i was conceived
and formed inside of my mothers
womb— as if i were formed
for him and only him; *yes.*"

as air gives life to lungs,
and rain life to the trees,
hope of a forever,
you and i,
gives life to my soul
and sets me free.

believe me,
sometimes i wish that i didn't
believe.

maybe life would go back
to normal then.
whatever that was.

…but the thing is,
since meeting him,
it is harder not to believe
than it is to believe.

how sweet the taste of
a romance is, that once was,
that we long and hope
again to be.

they would have you believe
that *l o v e* is dispensable; replaceable,
as if you could simply fall into
the arms of another
as so to land a cure.

but your soul's very cry is
proof that *l o v e* is a deeper,
more meaningful,
and sacred occurrence than that.

"i'll meet you in the promised land,"
he said.

"and how will i know that it is you?"

"you will know by the heat
begging to behold your skin —
as if a wall of fire is surrounding
you and glory dancing from within."

it is said "blessed are the hungry"
and having tasted life with and
without you,
i must agree.

for though the hunger pains
of losing you are harsh,
i know that the coming meal
would be
powerful enough to forever fill me.

the truth to the fairytales
that we grew up watching is this —
there is always some kind of
pain, seperation, or tribulation
that must first be overcome
before the princess receives the desires
of her heart.

life outside of the screen is no different.
remember this.

i would rather suffer in my
longing for you,
knowing that it is temporal,
than to be alleviated by a
mirage,
knowing that it could never
fully sustain me.

every second without you feels like eternity,
and every new breath,
like a thousand bricks placed on top of my lungs.

how much longer?

whether wise or foolish,
whether right or wrong,
hopeful or hopeless,

i choose you.

and if i had to face fear,
uncertainty,
and even wrath,

still, i'd choose you.

and if that's not *l o v e* ,
then i don't know what is.

when you promised never to leave,
i believed you.

still, i believe you.
because though your body is gone,
i feel your spirit every second of everyday,
here with me,
close to me,
keeping it's promise to me.

in a world founded on lies
and dependent on illusion,
it'd make sense that they
expect me to move on —
fake the way that i feel —
pretend that none of this
ever happened.

but as real as the flesh on my bones,
the heart beating wildly out of my
chest,
and this aching pain keeping me
from rest,

these feelings that i have for you
deserve their truth as well.

if we're being honest,
this was never going to
be an easy split.

when my eyes first
set their gaze upon you,
they bound knots
around the two of our
souls...
and i whispered to god,
"i am never letting this one go."

LOVE IN OTHER REALMS
199

finding myself,
having lost you,
has been my
life's greatest
catch twenty-two.

i'm tired of people telling me
that if it's messy
it is isn't good for me.

life is messy. yet here we are, living.
and what are we living for?

faith in better days. am i right?

and you and i, though messy now...
we can and we will find better days.

\

the truth is, *l o v e* touches us all a bit
differently.

for some,
it needs to feel light, like the wind.
for others, cleansing,
like the submersion of water or
grounding, like the soil of the earth.

and for the rest of us...
all consuming and transformative.

fire.

know this,
l o v e finds you when it finds you.
and it *always* finds you the way
that it has planned to find you.
it knew you before you knew of it.
it saw you before you ever
so much as caught a glimpse.

no amount of planning,
attempting to control it,
or searching for it
will change the outcome as to
when it finds you and *how* it finds you.

my best advice?
rest, until that day.

because when it finds you;
the way that it finds you...
your soul will have no other
choice but to abruptly awaken.
and you will be best prepared
if before hand
you took the time to rest.
so, *rest.*

"what if you're wrong about him?"
they asked.

"then i was wrong about him, but never my l o v e for him."

in his absence,
i rested…
not because it was
easy
or because it was
not worth the fight,
but because of
the wisdom that
i held close to my heart —
that there was a time
and a season for
everything under the sun;
a time to embrace
and a time to refrain;
a time to be silent
and a time to speak.

i rested…
not from defeat,
but from victory.

the truth is,
i'd always run after you —
even winded,
in agony,
and through all of life's
dark and unknown paths.

this life.
the last life.
the next life.

i'd always run after you.

until you, i had nothing to test my strength;
nothing worthy of my fight;
my breath;
my energy.

until you, there was no fight.
because until you...

there was no *l o v e .*

he is my dopamine;
my chemical messenger
effecting every way in
which i move.

so before you deem my
l o v e for him a sin,
won't you first consider
it to be biological?

i live for the days that i rise,
only half alive, to be revived,
midday by an act of random
discovery —
somehow the discoveries
always pointing their way
back to you.

a new genre of music;
a secret revealed in lyrics;
a key piece of information
to my journey —
my journey leading me
back home to you.

to rise, to be surprised,
and ultimately revived,
how typical the pattern
of our story.

if we knew the time and the place;
the way that *l o v e* works itself out...
there would be no room left for
the birth of magic.

and i must ask,
what is a world without magic?

you said, "people only watch magic
with the intent of figuring it out, but magic's
intent is to captivate, taking one's breath away,
for a moment, standing still in time."

and i want to tell you that i am not like them—
but the truth is
that i too am sleepless without the answers.
not necessarily the answers to magic,
but the answers to us.

and magic and us,
i feel have always been one and the same.

god's decree, you'll find your way back to me,
or i to you,
or us to us.
however it is to happen,
it is to happen.

LOVE IN OTHER REALMS
215

every day that i exist
is nothing more than my next
attempt at finding my way
back to you.

hope — a word that sounds harmless.
but for those of us who have held onto
it for long enough,
we know of it to be a double edged sword;
a matter of life or death.
a risk.

yet the same is to be said for hope as it is for *love* ,
the greatest risk is to have none at all.

my every breath
is a silent wish for you;
to have you,
to hold you,
and to give myself to you
in ways that i have *never*
given to another.

my very existence—
a never ending and
silent wish for you.

some things; some people,
they come painfully crashing into
our lives rather than peacefully
walking in.

and i believe that it *has to be this way.*
if not,
they would run the risk of failing
to awaken us to our purpose
and even greater, our destiny.

the promise of forever
is a beautiful thing,
is it not?

we must only be careful
not to allow it the justification
as to why we refuse to make the
moves here and now
beckoned by our heart and our soul.

why not here,
why not now?

you came into my life like a hurricane,
shaking me from side to side.
in the process
breaking me down,
yet also watering me.

and i thought, how could one person be both
the eye of the storm
just as much as they are the
surrounding winds?;
both the damage and the restoration?

nevertheless,
you are—
and i am forever changed.

he will find me once more in darkness,
or i will come for him
once my eyes have
caught hold of the light.

for neither of the two,
darkness nor light
decree a *l o v e*
other-worldly —
a *l o v e* as pure as his and i's.

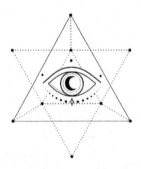

Acknowledgements:

First and foremost, to my pain. Though we have a love/hate relationship, it would be foolish of me not to acknowledge you and the good that has come from you. Thank you for helping me to forge my path in this world as a poet and as an artist; for pointing me more towards empathy, and for motivating me to press forward and to heal as much as I can in this lifetime. Though I pray one day to know you far less, you deserve to be acknowledged in the here and the now. So, thank you.

To the one who awakened my soul to a deeper love. They say that where there is great love, there too will also lie great pain. Now I know that to love you is to accept both. Though in many ways, life is harder for me now that you are gone, I have also learned, through you, that there is far more to this life than what I had previously known…and it is in this that I find my strength and my hope in tomorrow. I wish you and pray over you nothing but the best, and I thank you for the time that we did share and for gifting me with a story worth writing.

To my two children, Bradley and Noah. Though the poems in this book were not about the two of you, they are just as much for you, as they are for everyone else. Every second that I pour into poetry is a second that I pray God would transform into value for the two of you. In writing this book I am starting from square one, but my recurrent prayer is for God to allow me to build and leave behind a legacy for the two of you. As well, I pray that the two of you find and stay true to your purpose in life, no matter the way the world may tempt to deter you. You may take your time to rest, but don't you ever give up.

To my parents, for the breath of life and for the affirmations that I am both talented and capable of what it is that I put my mind to. If it were not for this and for the two of you providing for me, throughout life, I wouldn't be sitting here today with a chance so large —a chance at leaving a noticeable mark on this planet and a chance to pursue one of my life's greatest passions. Thank you.

To God, for the unspeakable; for what only my soul knows, but words fail to convey. For it all. I love you.

"I wondered how long it could last. Maybe someday,
years from now, if the pain would decrease to the point where
I could bear it, I would be able to look back on those few short
months that would always be the best
of my life. And if it were possible that the pain would
ever soften enough to allow me to do that, I was sure
that I would feel grateful for as much time as he
he'd given me.
More than I'd asked for, more than I deserved.
Maybe someday I'd be able to see it that way."

- Bella Swan, *New Moon.*

An acknowledgment from the author:

Illustrations found in this book have been obtained by various artists and have been purchased and licensed.

Page 95 was inspired by artist Bethaleil, and then recreated and added to. For the original piece of art and to check out more of this artist's work, look for him on Instagram under the username: @bethaleil

Thank you to all artists for helping me to create the aesthetic that I had always imagined for Love in Other Realms.
I am beyond grateful for this and for you.

with all of my love,

-melissa m combs